Princess Poppy
The Haunted
Holiday

written by Janey Louise Jones
Illustrated by Samantha Chaffey

THE HAUNTED HOLIDAY
A YOUNG CORGI BOOK 978 0 552 55597 5

First published in Great Britain by Young Corgi,
an imprint of Random House Children's Books

Young Corgi edition published 2007

1 3 5 7 9 10 8 6 4 2

Text copyright © Janey Louise Jones, 2007
Illustrations copyright © Random House Children's Books, 2007
Illustrations by Samantha Chaffey

Set in 14/21pt Bembo MT Schoolbook by
Falcon Oast Graphic Art Ltd.

Young Corgi Books are published by Random House Children's Books,
61–63 Uxbridge Road, London W5 5SA

www.**kids**at**randomhouse**.co.uk
www.princesspoppy.com

Addresses for companies within The Random House Group Limited
can be found at: www.randomhouse.co.uk/offices.htm

THE RANDOM HOUSE GROUP Limited Reg. No. 954009

A CIP catalogue record for this book is available from the British Library.

Printed and bound in Great Britain by
William Clowes Limited, Beccles, Suffolk

Princess Poppy
The Haunted Holiday

Check out Princess Poppy's website
to find out all about the other
books in the series

www.princesspoppy.com

Honeysuckle Cottage
(Poppy's House)

Poppy Field

Forget-Me-Not Cottage
Grandpa's House + office

Pot Cottage
Granny

Blossom
Bakehouse

Marigolds
General
Store

Cornsilk Castle
and
Courtyard

Village Hall

Sage's Vet Surgery

Post Office

Beehive
Beauty Salon

Riverside
stables

Barley Farm
The Meadowsweet's
House

River Swan

Honeypot Hill
Railway Station

To Camomile Cove
via Periwinkle Lane

W
N
E
S

Chapter One

"*Bonjour*, Honey!" called Poppy as her
best friend arrived with her suitcase and
backpack. "All ready for the holiday?"

"*Bonjour* to you too!" called Honey. "I've
been packed for days – I'm so excited.
How've the French lessons with your
grandpa been going?"

"*Très bien!*" said Poppy, showing off. "But
learning all the vocabulary is really difficult
and a bit boring. I love hearing all about
French history though. Grandpa makes

1

it sound so interesting – he's been telling me about the French Revolution. The last Queen of France was Marie Antoinette. She had hair as high as a top hat, and she wore dresses as fancy as a wedding dress every day! Grandpa told me that the French people decided that they didn't want to have kings and queens and princes and princesses any more so they just got rid of them. That's what the French Revolution was."

"Gosh, but why would anyone *not* want real princesses?" said Honey. "They must have been mad!"

Poppy shrugged her shoulders. She couldn't understand it either. "Who knows? It's such a terrible waste of beautiful palaces and tiaras and stuff," she said sadly.

"Exactly," agreed Honey.

"And guess what else Grandpa told me," said Poppy. "It's really gross!"

"What?" asked Honey, fascinated.

"People had their heads cut off by the revolutionaries!"

"I don't believe it. That's too cruel." Honey shuddered; she found it hard to imagine that such a thing could ever have happened. "I just can't wait to see my mum and dad again when we get to France," she said, deliberately changing the subject because she didn't want to hear any more about people having their heads chopped off. "It's been ages since I last saw them."

Poppy had always thought it strange
that Honey didn't live with her parents all
the time, but Honey had often explained
that her mum and dad had to travel a lot
for work. Honey's dad was a film producer
and her mum was a successful actress. After
they got married and had Honey, they had
planned to settle down in Honeypot Hill.
However, they needed to keep jetting about
the world for their work, so it was agreed
that Granny Bumble would keep Honey safe

at home. That way Honey was able to go to school and make friends there. Granny Bumble was a wonderful full-time parent, but that didn't stop Honey wishing that her mum and dad were around all the time.

Just then they heard the toot of a horn. It was Poppy's cousin Saffron and her husband David, the village vet. They were accompanying the girls on the flight: Saffron was off to the Paris fashion shows to get some inspiration for her new collection and David was going with her. Meanwhile Poppy and Honey were going to stay with Honey's parents in the historic Chateau de Lafayette, which they had rented for the whole summer. Daniel Bumble, Honey's dad, was working on new film ideas and thought that a couple of months in a French castle might inspire him! Saffron and David were going to join the girls at Chateau de Lafayette in the middle of the week, and

Poppy's family and Granny Bumble were
flying over a couple of days later for a long
weekend as Granny Bumble's birthday treat.

The girls climbed into David's ear and
waved goodbye to Mum, Dad, the twins,
Grandpa and Granny Bumble.

"I can't wait to see Chateau de Lafayette,"
said Saffron on the way to the airport. "I just
love the atmosphere in old buildings. What's
it like, Honey?"

"Well, I haven't actually been there before,
but Mum and Dad told me that it's hundreds
of years old and really, really big, and it has
a really interesting history. I hope nothing

too horrible happened there though!" said
Honey, remembering what Poppy had told
her earlier. "It used to belong to a French
noble family called the de Lafayettes," she
continued, "and my mum says it looks like a
giant fairy castle."

"Maybe it's haunted," said David, making
a spooky woooo-woooo noise.

"David, just concentrate on the driving!"
said Saffron.

"Just teasing," he smiled. "Actually, I wish
I was coming straight to the castle instead
of being dragged round the fashion shows.
It'll be so much more fun than admiring

stick-insect models in boring black outfits all day long."

Even though she knew David had been teasing them, Poppy couldn't get what he had said out of her mind – what if the castle *was* haunted? It would be so exciting.

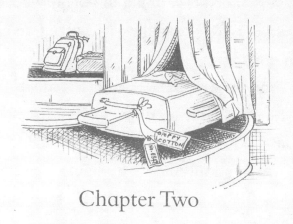

Chapter Two

When they got to the airport, they headed straight for the check-in desk and handed their luggage over. Poppy was amazed when her pink pull-along suitcase disappeared on a black conveyor belt through two plastic curtains.

"Don't worry," said Saffron. "It has a label with your name and flight number on it. You'll get it back when we arrive in France!"

Before long they had all boarded the aircraft. Honey had flown lots of times and she explained everything to Poppy, who was both nervous and excited about going on a plane.

"You have to wear a seatbelt and we'll get a meal halfway through the journey. The food is so cute – it's just like having a doll's tea party! And it's brilliant when you take off. You leave the ground behind and go up and up into the clouds," said Honey excitedly.

"I just can't see how this great big aeroplane can actually get off the ground!" Poppy said, looking worried.

"I don't really get it either," confessed Honey, "but it always does!"

They stowed their bags away in the overhead lockers, settled down in their seats and strapped themselves in. Soon they were whizzing along the runway at top speed and, as if by magic, the plane rose effortlessly into the air, leaving the runway far below.

"Wow!" said Poppy, peering out of the
window to see the tiny fields and hedgerows.
"I still don't get why we don't fall out of
the sky."

Saffron smiled.

Just then the captain of the aircraft came on the loud-speaker to address everyone.

"Hello, ladies and gentlemen, boys and girls. This is your captain speaking. As you can see, I have now switched off the 'Fasten Seatbelts' sign and you are free to move around the aircraft. We are flying at an altitude of fifty thousand feet and at a speed of five hundred and sixty miles per hour. We will arrive in Paris at ten thirty a.m. local time. The weather conditions there are very warm and muggy at thirty degrees Centigrade. We do hope you enjoy your flight today, and if there is anything we can do to assist your on-board comfort, please do not hesitate to ask one of the cabin crew."

Soon the air stewardesses arrived with a trolley crammed full of dinky little meal trays.

"That must be *such* a great job," Poppy said to Honey. "Maybe that's what we should do when we grow up. We could travel the world!"

"That would be cool," replied Honey, nodding in agreement.

Poppy and Honey spent almost the whole flight spreading little pats of butter onto impossibly cute little rolls with incredibly flimsy plastic knives. Then they wiped their hands with the wet-wipe, tidied up their trays and strapped themselves back in, all ready for landing.

After what seemed like a very short time the plane zoomed down onto the runway in France. They disembarked, went through passport control, then collected their luggage and headed for the 'Arrivals' area. Because

Saffron and David were going straight to
the centre of Paris from the airport, Honey's
mum and dad had arranged for the girls
to be picked up by Chateau de Lafayette's
butler and chauffeur, Pierre, so they were
all looking out for him as they emerged
with their luggage. Even though they had
never met him before, they spotted him
immediately because he was carrying a
board which read:

The girls kissed Saffron and David goodbye
until later in the week and followed Pierre to
the car park. He put their cases in the boot
while the two girls settled down in the back

seat of the big old-fashioned car. Pierre got into the front, started the engine and they set off.

"I feel like a film star," said Poppy as she slipped on her sunglasses. "Just like your mum!"

Honey smiled and put on her sunglasses too and the two girls posed happily in the back of the car, pretending they were famous.

They began to leave the city behind and Poppy had butterflies of excitement inside her as they drove through magnificent rolling countryside with rich dark-green forests. It looked like scenery from a story book. But

nothing could have prepared them for the
grandeur of Chateau de Lafayette. Before
long they were approaching some huge
black wrought-iron gates.

"This must be the castle," said Honey as
the gates opened magically and they swept
inside the secret world behind the high walls.
"I hope it really is a fairytale castle!"

"Here we are," said Pierre. "This is
Chateau de Lafayette. Isn't it beautiful?"

Chapter Three

Honey's parents were waiting to greet them
on the steps of the magnificent old castle.
Poppy thought it looked just like a fancy
iced wedding cake, with its pillars and towers
and pale-cream stone frontage. There was
a beautiful fountain in front, which was
surrounded by the huge, sweeping driveway,
and to one side was an enormous stable block.
Honey ran towards her mum and dad and
gave them a huge hug, while Poppy held back,
then kissed them both politely on each cheek.

Honey's mum was lovely. She was American and she dressed like a bit of a hippy. Poppy thought she was very pretty and glamorous, with her beautiful rich brown skin and dark curly hair like Honey's. But like all little  girls, Poppy thought her own mother was the loveliest in the whole wide world.

"How lovely to see you, girls!" said Mrs Bumble. "We're going to have such a wonderful time. There are so many fun things to do here: walks and picnics, swimming, boating on the lake, exploring the castle, riding and masses more."

"Jasmine's right," smiled Honey's dad. "This is going to be the best holiday ever, although I'm afraid I've got a lot of work to do so I won't be able to join in the fun as much as

I'd hoped. In fact, I've got a phone call to make right now so I'll leave you girls to it. Happy exploring, and don't get lost!"

"Where's the pool, Mum?" asked Honey. "We've been having swimming lessons at school all term and I want to show you how much I've learned. I don't even need my floats any more."

"It's at the back, in the courtyard, darling, but there's no hurry. Why don't I show you around first?"

"Yes please," chorused the girls.

"I'll give you a tour of the whole place so you can find your way around without me," explained Mrs Bumble just as Pierre bustled in

with Poppy and Honey's cases. "Oh, Pierre, thank you so much," she said to him. "Please can you take them up to the *Chambre de Charlotte* – we'll unpack later. Come on, girls, let's go exploring and after that we'll have a nice cool drink by the pool."

The girls gazed about in amazement as they entered the huge picture gallery.

All of Honeysuckle Cottage could fit in here, thought Poppy.

Chateau de Lafayette was not exactly beautiful – it was much too grand and historical for that – but it was certainly very impressive. As Poppy looked around, totally in awe of her surroundings, something made a

shiver run down her spine. It was definitely a bit eerie, but maybe that was just because it was so big and unfamiliar. There were sculptures, and tapestries hanging on the walls, and fancy plasterwork which Honey's mum said was called stucco. The walls were lined with portraits of elegant men and fine-looking women, whose eyes seemed to follow them wherever they went, as well as pretty little girls with ringlets. The children in the portraits were all beautifully dressed and made Poppy wish that she'd lived in a time when people wore fancy clothes every day. They all wore frilled satin dresses with pretty, wide sleeves and square necklines edged with lace. Some even wore exquisite beribboned bonnets over their curly hair.

"Chateau de Lafayette was owned by a French noble family for hundreds of years," explained Honey's mum as they walked through the gallery. "It was built by the first

Marquis de Lafayette nearly four hundred years ago. Here is the beautiful wife of the fourth Marquis, Marguerite de Lafayette, who vanished during the French Revolution" – she pointed to the grand portraits hanging on the wall to their right – "and here is her husband, Étienne, the fourth Marquis."

Then she turned to another picture, which was hanging between the Marquis and his wife. "This one here is of their beloved youngest daughter, Charlotte."

The little girl looked as though she was about the same age as Poppy and Honey. She was wearing a fancy powder-blue satin dress and holding a posy of violets, which Honey's mother told them denoted sadness.

"Poor little Charlotte – the locals say her ghost paces the castle at night looking for her mother and singing a lullaby but I haven't heard or seen anything. It's just gossip – I don't believe a word of it," she

went on firmly, and continued with the tour.

But Poppy and Honey couldn't take their eyes off the portrait of Charlotte de Lafayette. And as they looked at it, they both felt terribly sorry for the little girl in the beautiful dress. In her mind's eye Poppy could see this family living in the grand castle centuries before; she was desperate to know more about them.

"What happened to the de Lafayette

family in the end?" she asked as she caught up with Honey's mum.

"You know, I really don't know," replied Mrs Bumble. "There are hundreds of books in the library – maybe you'll be able to find out some more about them by doing a little reading."

During the tour of the house they met the housekeeper, who was polishing the grand wooden staircase.

"This is Mathilde," Mrs Bumble told them. "I don't know what I'd do without her. She keeps everything running so smoothly. She's Pierre's sister."

Both girls smiled at Mathilde and she smiled back at them. Poppy thought she looked very kind and slightly familiar, although she couldn't work out why.

On the upper level they walked along wood-panelled corridor after wood-panelled corridor. Poppy tried to count the doors they passed but soon gave up – there were too many. At last they stopped at a door which had a huge key hanging from the lock.

"This is your room, girls," said Honey's mum. "Mathilde told me that.it used to belong to little Charlotte. I think it's the prettiest room in the whole castle."

The girls gasped. Imagine actually sleeping in Charlotte de Lafayette's bedroom! They stepped inside, desperate to see what the room looked like, and they were not disappointed. It was huge! There were two great big beds with gilt and brocade headboards, and an enormous window framed by heavy red velvet drapes, which overlooked a fountain that was even more spectacular than the one in the drive. They also had a view of a courtyard which was filled with statues and roses, and at the end of a spectacular terrace was the swimming pool. Beyond that they could see a pretty lake and some dark green woods which sealed Chateau de Lafayette from the outside world. The room was furnished with beautiful antique furniture that looked as if it had come straight out of a museum, and there were more portraits hanging on the oak-panelled walls. Poppy read out the names at the bottom of the portraits with interest, wondering who they all were.

"Wow! This place is amazing," said Honey. "I can't believe we're actually staying here."

"Why not change into your swimming things?" suggested Honey's mum as the girls tried to take in their spectacular surroundings. "We can unpack later. Shall we

meet at the pool in about five minutes? You bring your towels and pool robes and I'll bring some refreshments – you girls must be hungry and thirsty after your journey."

"OK, Mum. We'll see you there," replied Honey. "Can we lock the door when we leave the room?"

"Yes, if you like, but really there's no need. No one here's going to steal your things!" laughed Mrs Bumble. "Make sure you don't lose the key though – otherwise you'll be locked out and there isn't a spare."

Chapter Four

"This castle is massive! I'm never going to remember where everything is," said Honey as they headed for the pool.

"I wonder if Charlotte ever got lost," replied Poppy.

"She probably grew up here so it wouldn't have seemed as huge to her – it was all she would have known," said Honey.

"Yeah, I suppose so." Poppy smiled as she skipped down the stairs.

When they eventually found the pool,

there was no sign of Honey's mum so they decided to put their stuff down and go for a wander around. The very first thing that caught Poppy's eye was a small dark alley to the right of the pool house: she simply could not resist a peek!

"Come on, Honey, let's see what's down there."

Reluctantly Honey followed. At the end of the alley, which smelled very damp and musty, they came upon an old wooden gate set in a crumbling stone wall. Poppy peeped

through a crack in the gate and saw that it
led to a pretty little garden with flowerbeds
all around the edges and a child's swing
hanging from a tree. But as the girls went
into the garden, they noticed that the swing
was gently swinging to and fro as if there
was someone on it – although the garden
was empty.

"Did you see that?" asked Honey.

"Yeah, it's weird!" replied Poppy, a shiver
running down her spine. "It's not even windy
today."

"This is really creepy." Honey shuddered.
"I'm going back to the pool – are you coming?"

At that moment, much to their relief, they heard Mrs Bumble calling them. They ran down the dark pathway towards the terrace as fast as their feet would take them.

Honey's mum had laid out a delicious picnic for them to have after their swim. There was a jug of sparkling fruit punch, crusty French bread spread with creamy butter, along with delicious green apples and yummy-looking smelly cheeses. There was also a plate of fancy cakes and pastries, which looked scrumptious.

It was a very hot day so the water was
particularly refreshing and before long both
girls had forgotten how spooked they'd felt
earlier. Poppy splashed around confidently
while Honey showed her mum how much
her swimming had improved. There was
a slide at one end of the pool and after
dashing down it several times feet first, then
head first, Poppy wrapped herself in her
towel, put on her sunglasses and began to
nibble on the picnic.

After a while Pierre appeared. "Madame Bumble, there is a telephone call for you from Granny Bumble," he told Honey's mum.

"Ah, thank you, Pierre. I'll be there in a minute," she replied.

The two girls lay by the pool and smothered their skin in sun cream, but even though it was very hot, the sun was struggling to break through the heavy grey clouds. Suddenly a really black cloud came over Chateau de Lafayette and the girls felt heavy droplets of rain on their skin. They grabbed their things and started running back towards the castle. As they made their

way through the huge French windows, a
crash of thunder sounded in the distance and
the heavens opened, the rain falling in heavy
sheets – they'd made it inside just in time.

When they got back to their bedroom,
Honey put the big old key in the lock and
turned the handle. But on entering the
room, they immediately saw that all their

belongings had been unpacked and laid out
neatly on the beds. The girls looked at each
other nervously.

"Who did that? We had the key all the
time, didn't we?" said Poppy.

"Um, yes. And I'm sure Mum said
there wasn't a spare," said Honey, looking
apprehensively around the huge room.
"Maybe David was right about this place
being haunted."

"Perhaps the ghost of little Charlotte
unpacked our stuff for us. I'd much rather
it was her than the man in that picture,"

said Poppy as she pointed to the portrait of a wicked-looking man whose beady eyes appeared to be looking right at her! "Maybe there was a ghost on the swing too. That would explain why it was moving—"

Comte de Grace

"Shush, Poppy. You're scaring me. This place is way too spooky," said Honey quietly.

When the girls were dressed again, they went over to the window to watch the storm. The sky was black except for the periodic

sparks of lightning shooting across it, and
the thunder rumbled in the distance like
an angry god beating a drum. Just then,
the thunder clapped right above them and
the lights began to flicker, casting spooky
shadows in the room. Both girls, already
quite jumpy, screamed and grabbed hold of
each other for comfort.

As the afternoon wore on, the storm
showed no sign of abating, and Poppy and
Honey were getting more and more spooked,

so they decided to settle down and play a game with Honey's dad. They felt much safer with a grown-up around. The three of them gathered in the library and set out a game of Cluedo, which was Honey's favourite game – she always wanted to be Miss Scarlett. As they played, the wind howled around the castle ramparts, the rain pitter-pattered on the ancient windows and every so often the lights would flicker off then on again, just as they had earlier.

"I'm going down to the kitchen to fetch some candles, girls," said Honey's dad. "I've a feeling this storm might bring the power lines right down and we can't play Cluedo in the dark, can we? I'll be back in a minute. No cheating!"

"Let's look at some of these books while we're waiting for your dad, Honey," Poppy suggested. "Maybe we'll find out some more about the de Lafayettes and whether or not this castle is really haunted."

"I think I'm just going to sit here – I don't want to think about ghosts," replied Honey.

Poppy pulled out a beautiful leather-bound book, and even though she couldn't read the French, as she flicked through the pages, she was transported to another world. She imagined that she was living in Chateau de Lafayette in the time of Charlotte. She was brought back to reality rather suddenly by the sound of the heavy library door creaking open. Poppy was so startled that she jumped and let out a squeal, as did Honey, who couldn't bear to look at the door, terrified of what she might see on the other side . . .

Chapter Five

"What's all the squealing for?" asked Mr
Bumble as he came back into the library
with a candle in each hand.

"It's just this storm, Dad," explained
Honey.

They didn't want to tell him that they
thought the castle might be haunted.
Somehow they wanted to find out more
about Charlotte de Lafayette for themselves
– and they didn't want him to think they
were being silly.

"It'll be fine, girls. It's just a summer storm. It'll be over soon and you'll be able to play outside again," he replied as he put the candles down on the table and they got back to their game.

After they had finished and Honey had won, the girls went back up to their room. Poppy decided to take the book she'd found in the library with her so that she could take a closer look at it and see whether she could decipher any of the words.

"Supper's in the dining room at seven thirty sharp," Honey's dad called up to them. "Don't be late or Jean-Paul, the cook, will be cross! He hates it if his food is spoiled."

"OK, Dad," Honey replied. "See you later."

She settled down to finish the necklace she was making for Granny Bumble's birthday present and Poppy curled up in an armchair and studied the book in more detail. At seven o'clock Honey decided that it was time to get ready for supper – she hated being late for anything.

"What are you going to wear, Poppy?" she asked.

"I just wish I had a long frilly dress to wear," replied Poppy as she looked longingly at the portraits, "but I suppose I'll just wear my red dress and matching cardigan."

Honey slipped on a yellow and green striped dress, ballet pumps and a white cardigan, and sat on her bed waiting for Poppy to get dressed. Then they made their way down to supper in the enormous formal dining room. It had oak-panelled walls adorned with reminders of a bygone era and the heritage of the de Lafayettes: shields and swords from the medieval period, when the de Lafayettes were noble knights; embroidered tapestries depicting battle scenes; plus a huge dinner service engraved with the family emblem, a love-heart and a sword.

Supper was a grand affair and Honey's mum and dad had dressed up too. Mrs Bumble looked especially wonderful in a floor-length halter-neck black dress with thin gold stripes. The food was delicious, and as they ate, Honey's dad talked to them about French food, customs and history. The two friends listened intently.

"Thank you for the yummy meal, Mrs Bumble," said Poppy politely as she wiped her mouth with her heavy linen napkin.

"Oh, Poppy, don't thank me – I can't boil an egg. It's all down to Jean-Paul – Pierre and Mathilde's brother."

"Imagine a whole family working at the same place. Isn't that nice?" said Poppy.

"Yes, it is rather sweet," agreed Mrs Bumble, "and they all work so well together. Now, it's time you two went off to bed. You need to get a good night's sleep. I'm going to be tied up with preparations for Granny Bumble's surprise party tomorrow so I've asked Mathilde if she'll take you along on her trip to the market in the village, and then in the afternoon maybe you could go riding or swimming – whatever you like."

The girls looked thrilled.

"Night-night!" they chorused.

"I don't think I'll sleep a wink," said Poppy as they made their way upstairs. "I wish I hadn't brought a Nancy Drew Mystery for my bedtime reading. I'm all creeped out as it is. What if Charlotte's ghost paces about our room during the night!"

"Stop it, Poppy. You're scaring me – I won't sleep now either," wailed Honey and grabbed hold of her friend's hand.

Just then, as they were
halfway up the huge
staircase, they heard a
great boom of thunder
and the lights cut out
completely. They were
left in inky blackness,
with only flashes of
lightning illuminating
the landing.

"Help!" screamed
Poppy. "What's going
on?"

"I don't know, but I'm
scared. I want my dad!"
wailed Honey. "What
are we going to do?"

"What do you think
Charlotte would have
done?" asked Poppy,
sounding braver than

she felt. "They wouldn't have had any electricity when she lived here all those years ago."

"Um, I suppose not," replied Honey, feeling slightly better. "They would have used candles all the time after dark, wouldn't they? Just like we did earlier."

Poppy nodded. She was trying her best to recover from the shock and was just imagining what every night must have been like for the de Lafayettes, when her thoughts were interrupted.

"Wait there, girls! Don't worry, I'm coming," called Honey's dad. "I'll bring you some candles to guide you to your room."

They followed him up the stairs, and when they reached their bedroom, he put the candles on their bedside tables.

"As soon as you are ready to sleep, you must blow out the candles. I'll check on you in a bit. Night-night! Sleep tight!"

Poppy and Honey were much too excited
to sleep. Instead of getting ready for bed,
they decided to have a really good look
around to see whether they could discover
anything more about the little girl who had
slept in that room over two hundred years
before. Having been scared out of their wits
on their way to bed, they were gradually
getting used to the candlelight and even
started to enjoy it. They felt just like they
were living in olden times.

"Come on, Honey. Bring your candle over
to the big desk. I bet we'll find some clues in
there," said Poppy.

Honey thought her friend had been
reading too much Nancy Drew, but she went
over anyway – she was as keen as Poppy
to find out more about the de Lafayettes,
especially Charlotte.

Most of the furniture had nothing but dust
inside, but finally, much to her delight, Poppy

struck lucky in a little child's desk.

Having searched through the drawers, she tried the latch to a little compartment, but it was shut tight.

"Honey, look!" she whispered urgently. "I've found something here but I can't get into it. I think it's locked."

"Do you remember that film we saw – when the girl used a hair grip to pick a lock?" Honey asked her.

"Oh yeah, let's try that," said Poppy.

After a great deal of fiddling and twisting it finally fell open to reveal an exquisite wooden box, inlaid with gold letters.

"Wow! This must have belonged to Charlotte de Lafayette," exclaimed Poppy. "Look at the initials."

She carefully lifted the lid of the box and they looked inside. It contained a gold locket, a silver rattle and a folded document, which seemed to be a map of Chateau de Lafayette. Beneath all these was an envelope sealed with wax.

"Wow! This must be a letter from Charlotte to her mum!" Poppy said as she picked up the envelope.

"It must be – but look, it's still sealed: maybe no one except Charlotte has ever read it," said Honey.

"We'd better not break the seal – anyway, we can't read French that well," Poppy said sensibly.

"Well, let's open the locket and see what's inside," suggested Honey.

Poppy picked up the locket and gently prised the two oval-shaped halves apart. One side was empty, but on the other she recognized a tiny portrait of Marguerite de Lafayette, Charlotte's mother.

Then they took a closer look at the map. As Poppy unfolded it, they both saw that it was no ordinary map. It included many things they didn't recognize.

"Look, there are three places marked with a red love-heart. Do you think these were places Charlotte especially loved?" asked Poppy.

"Let's try to find them," said Honey.

There was a room at the top of the turret, which looked to them like it was above their bedroom. The garden with the swing was also marked, as well as the forest beyond the lake.

"Do you think these might be secret passages?" wondered Honey, pointing to some more strange marks on the map.

"They must be," replied Poppy. "How exciting! It looks as if our bedroom has one behind it, but there are no doors in here except the one we use, are there?"

"I've not seen any others but it might be a trick door. Maybe we should take a more careful look," said Honey.

They moved pieces of furniture and huge pictures and peeked behind curtains and lamps, but there was no sign of a secret door anywhere. Then, fumbling in the dark, Poppy dropped a vase on her toes and let out a squeal. Luckily it wasn't damaged, but all of a sudden they heard footsteps marching purposefully towards their door. Poppy felt hot and panicky. She imagined the creepy Comte de Grace from the portrait coming to get them . . .

As the door opened, both girls leaped onto Honey's bed and hid under the covers.

"Are you OK, girls?" asked the familiar

voice of Honey's dad as he came in.

Poppy and Honey breathed a huge sigh of relief and peeped over the duvet.

"We're just going to sleep, Dad," said Honey.

"OK." He kissed both girls goodnight and blew out their candles. "But you'll sleep much better in separate beds."

When he had gone, the two girls shivered.

"Can I stay in your bed, Honey?" asked Poppy.

"Yes please," agreed Honey, glad that she

wasn't the only one who was frightened.

As the girls began to drop off to sleep, still wearing their clothes, they were disturbed by a lovely voice coming from above them. It was a child singing a lullaby.

"That must be Charlotte!" said Honey.

The singing soon stopped and, curiously enough, the girls felt soothed rather than frightened by it: before long they were fast asleep.

Chapter Six

Amazingly, the sky was bright and clear
when the girls came down the next morning.
Breakfast was served in the huge kitchen in
the basement. There was a vast range-style
cooker and wooden dressers displaying a
selection of copper pots and jelly moulds.
Poppy and Honey sat at a long wooden
table with Honey's mum, chatting merrily
and spreading homemade raspberry jam on
warm, buttery croissants. It seemed silly that
they had been so afraid the night before.

Everything was perfectly calm now, but they couldn't stop thinking about the things that had happened. It was all so mysterious and exciting!

Just as they were finishing their breakfast, Mathilde came to tell them that it was time to go to the village.

"Can we just get our bags from the bedroom please, Mathilde?" asked Honey.

"Of course. I'll wait for you by the van," replied Mathilde kindly.

Poppy and Honey ran all the way back to their bedroom, but as soon as they were away from the calm and safe environment of the kitchen, they both felt rather jumpy. They turned the key in the lock and the door swung open by itself. There seemed to be a cold wind moving through the room, followed by a banging sound near the window. The girls crept in gingerly. They were apprehensive rather than frightened,

but desperate to find out what was going on.
As they looked around, everything seemed
normal. Charlotte's pretty little box was
still on the desk and their own things were
precisely where they'd left them. Then, at
exactly the same moment, both girls noticed
that a small, old-fashioned doll had been
placed on Honey's bed.

    "Where did that come from?" Poppy
wondered.
    "Search me," replied Honey nervously.
"Look – there's a scrap of paper on the floor
too."
    "What does it say?" asked Poppy.

Honey read out the words: "*Je suis Charlotte de Lafayette.*"

"That means it's really true – the castle is haunted by Charlotte. Do you think she wants to be friends?" asked Poppy, hoping that she would be able to make friends with a real ghost. "This is so amazing, Honey. We're on holiday in a real haunted castle. I can't wait to tell everyone back in Honeypot Hill."

"Well, I just can't wait to get out of this room," replied Honey. "Let's go and find Mathilde."

They grabbed their sequinned shoulder bags and ran off to meet the housekeeper.

As the little van set off for the village, Poppy noticed a very long shopping list lying on the dashboard.

"That's a lot of food," she said to Mathilde.

"Yes, I know. Jean-Paul is going to make

many delicious dishes for when Saffron
and David arrive. And, of course, for the
fantastic party we are throwing for Monsieur
Bumble's mother." Mathilde smiled at them.

The girls were amazed by the lively and
exciting market. In addition to the neat stalls
selling bread, cheese, ham and fruit, there
were lots of other attractions.

"Look at the street artist!" exclaimed
Poppy, seeing a man sitting with his easel.

"Wow! A puppet show too," said Honey.

People were cycling in and out of the stalls
and street cafés, laughing and calling out to
each other. The air smelled of freshly baked
bread and strong coffee. Mathilde bought
the girls an apple each, as well as an almond
pastry, and told them all about the produce
on each stall. Poppy and Honey noticed
that the stallholders greeted Mathilde with
great warmth and respect. One cheeky-
looking man on a vegetable stall winked at

her and said something
in French. The only
words that Poppy
could make out were
Charlotte de Lafayette.
Mathilde told him
to 'shush', which
made Poppy wish she'd paid a bit more
attention to Grandpa's French lessons.

By the time they'd finished, the van was
full to bursting with all the wonderful
things they'd bought – from smelly local
cheeses and crusty bread to wine and even
champagne!

Back at Chateau de Lafayette, Poppy
and Honey helped unload the van and the
rest of the day passed uneventfully. They
swam and sunbathed and had a picnic
lunch by the pool with Honey's parents. In
fact, things were so normal that both girls
were beginning to think they'd imagined

everything. That night they fell asleep straight away – this time in their own beds!

The next morning the weather was even more beautiful and Poppy and Honey were desperate to get outside after breakfast.

"Can we go boating on the big lake today?" Poppy asked Mr Bumble.

"What a great idea," he replied. "I'm not much of a rower, I'm afraid, but I'm sure Pierre wouldn't mind taking you out – he's an expert! I'll give him a call now and ask him to meet you by the lake in half an hour."

As Poppy and Honey sat in the sunshine, waiting for Pierre, they looked out over the still, glassy lake. Soon Pierre arrived. He helped them into life-jackets and then into the boat. He climbed in, sat facing them and began to row out into the middle of the lake.

"See the ancient hunting wood ahead?" he said. "Many centuries ago the de Lafayettes hid in there when the revolutionaries came to capture them. It must have been very frightening."

Suddenly, as Pierre was telling them about more of the de Lafayette's history, Poppy's eye was drawn by movement in the woods on the far side of the lake. She was sure this was one of the spots marked with a love-heart on Charlotte's map.

"Honey, look over there," she whispered. "Can you see anything, or anyone?"

All at once the two girls saw a small figure running between the trees, stopping every now and then to pick violets from the forest floor. She wore a long powder-blue dress and her hair was in ringlets.

Poppy gasped. "It's Charlotte de Lafayette! Just like in the portrait – she's even picking the flowers she holds in the picture and

wearing the exact same dress!" she said.

"What are you girls whispering about? Aren't you interested in my stories?" asked Pierre.

"Um, it's not that we're not interested," replied Poppy. "It's just that we thought we saw someone in the woods. Can we go and have a look please?"

"Oh, girls, don't be silly! Your eyes are playing tricks on you. It is probably just a rabbit or a fox. There are many animals in the woods. But we should be getting back now, I'm afraid. I have work to do," said Pierre as he turned the little boat round and started rowing them back.

He helped Poppy and Honey out of the boat and the three of them walked up towards the stables together.

"Now," said Pierre, "why don't you go and see all the ponies – you can groom them, if you like. I have work to do on the cars – I'll be able to keep an eye on you from that building over there where they're kept."

"I don't understand why he doesn't want us to go into the woods," said Honey as soon as he was out of earshot.

"Me neither, but we'll find out," replied Poppy. "Quick – follow me. He's not looking!"

She ran all the way round the lake, with Honey trotting beside her. When they reached the edge of the woods, they stopped and tiptoed forward. "Come on, Honey," Poppy said. "We have to go inside if we want to meet Charlotte."

"But I'm scared," confessed Honey.

Suddenly there was a rustling noise in the trees beyond them. Honey grabbed Poppy's hand.

"It'll just be a fox," said Poppy bravely.

"No, it's something bigger. What if it's a bear or a wild boar or something?" wailed Honey.

Suddenly they both spotted the large figure of Pierre: he was heading straight for them!

"Girls, what are you doing here? Please come back to the stables," he said when he caught up with them.

Poppy and Honey reluctantly followed Pierre. But both of them were now more convinced than ever that they had seen a ghost in the woods and that Pierre was keeping something from them. They were desperate to know the truth.

Chapter Seven

Poppy and Honey spent the afternoon in the stables, petting and grooming the ponies. They were so engrossed in what they were doing that they didn't realize Pierre had gone out in the car. Nor did they hear him return, even though the car made a noise on the crunchy gravel. But suddenly they were both startled by the sound of footsteps approaching.

"*Aaaaarghhh!* Who's that?" squealed Honey.

"What if it's the ghost of that creepy Comte?" exclaimed Poppy.

The stable door creaked open and the girls were paralysed with fear. But when they finally dared to look up, they saw that there was nothing to be frightened of. The footsteps belonged to David and Saffron. They had come from Paris already! The girls began to breathe normally again.

"Hello, girls!" said Saffron. "How are you?"

Both Poppy and Honey gave her a huge hug.

"What's all this about?" she asked, surprised by how pleased the girls were to see her.

"We've got so much to tell you. So many weird things have been happening here. You know how David was teasing us about the castle being haunted? Well, it really is! By the

lonely spirit of Charlotte de Lafayette. We've heard her in the night and we've just seen her in the woods!" explained Poppy breathlessly.

"Calm down, Poppy. Let's go inside and you can tell me all about it," said Saffron, taking both girls by the hand and leading them towards the castle. "Maybe you could give us a tour at the same time."

After the tour they all went to find Mr and Mrs Bumble to let them know that Saffron and David had arrived. They found them in the library.

"It's great to see you. How was Paris?" asked Honey's mum.

"Brilliant, thanks! I've got so many ideas for new designs now," replied Saffron.

Soon the adults were chatting away merrily. Poppy and Honey thought it very dull, so they decided to go up to their bedroom. Everything looked normal at

first, but then Poppy noticed that one of
the big heavy drapes wasn't hanging as it
should. When they went to investigate, they
discovered that it was snagged on something.
It was a secret door disguised as panelling
and it was ajar!

"This must be the passage we saw on the
map. I wonder where it goes," said Honey.

"Pass me the map," said Poppy. "Look at
the love-heart Charlotte has marked here.
There seems to be a room at the top of the
turret which is connected to this passageway.
Let's investigate."

"OK, but only if you go first," Honey replied nervously.

The girls found themselves on a winding stone staircase that went right to the top of the turret. It was cobwebby and draughty. Although they were frightened, their curiosity was greater than their fear. As they climbed, they could hear noises above them. It sounded to Poppy and Honey like a child playing. Suddenly they heard footsteps coming from lower down, racing to catch up with them. Poppy's throat went dry. Both girls grabbed each other's hands and froze. The footsteps stopped and they looked down. It was Mathilde.

"Girls, what are you doing here?" she asked.

"Um, well, when we came back to our room, we found a secret door in the panelling and . . . um . . . it was open, so we decided to explore. We were just curious," explained Poppy quietly.

"Go back to your room at once. This part of the castle is private," said Mathilde.

The girls were very embarrassed to be caught snooping around, but also rather surprised at Mathilde's harsh tone. She had been so kind to them before. As they headed back to their room, Mathilde carried on towards the top of the turret, which both girls thought rather odd.

"Well, at least we know how Charlotte's ghost has been getting into our room," said Honey.

"Ghosts don't need doors, silly. They can float through walls," laughed Poppy.

"Maybe it's not a ghost who's been coming into our room then," replied Honey.

"But then who was on the swing, and who did we see in the woods?" asked Poppy, unwilling to give up on the idea that the ghost of the little girl wanted to be their friend.

"I don't know," said Honey. "But I hope it's not a ghost. They spook me out."

That night Poppy and Honey slept holding hands in Honey's bed, with the light on. The little doll that had been left in their room lay between them.

Chapter Eight

Saffron was already at the big kitchen table when the girls appeared next morning.

"David is helping Jasmine with the party plans," said Saffron. "Why don't we go down to the lake and do some sketching? After that I could give you a tennis lesson, or perhaps we could go for a swim."

The girls nodded. "Can we go for a walk in the woods too?" asked Poppy.

"Oh, that sounds lovely," replied Saffron.

"I think there were some tennis rackets in

the entrance hall," said Poppy. "I'll go and
have a look and meet you back here in a
minute."

The huge hall was flooded with sunlight.
Poppy was just making her way across to
the corner where she had seen the rackets
and balls when something made her look up
at the staircase above. There,
peering over the banister,
was the girl with the
ringlets and the powder-
blue dress. She waved at
Poppy, smiling merrily,
and then ran off.

"*Bonjour!*" gasped Poppy. "*Comment t'appelles-tu?*"

But the girl had vanished.

Poppy knew she really had seen Charlotte this time – it was definitely not her imagination. She was not like an apparition, she was just like a normal child. And what's more, she didn't look at all unhappy.

No one is going to believe that I've seen her, thought Poppy, so she decided to keep it to herself.

She went back to the kitchen with the rackets and then they made their way down to the lake with Saffron. She spread a rug on the grass and began to unpack sketch pads, pencils and paints. Poppy and Honey fed stale bread to the ducks and chatted away happily. Suddenly they noticed that Saffron was staring into the woods in a trance. It was as though she had seen a ghost. They followed her gaze . . . and saw that it was

83

the child again – the ghost-child, dancing
through the violets as before. She was waving
across to them, almost teasing them. They
all waved back like robots, hardly believing
what they were seeing.

"Now do you believe me, Saffron?" asked
Poppy.

"Yes," said Saffron softly. "Yes, I do. It must
be Charlotte de Lafayette."

They were all very quiet for the rest of the
morning. They went back for lunch with
Honey's parents and David, but none of
them spoke of what they had seen. It was
as if the magic would be destroyed if they
discussed it.

"Honey," whispered Poppy when the adults had gone into the library for coffee, "I just saw Mathilde go out in her van. Why don't we go exploring again? We won't get caught this time."

Honey nodded nervously. They just had to see what was in the turret.

Once again Poppy led the way. At the top of the stairs they arrived at a closed door. She pushed it open, and there before them was a gorgeously decorated room, filled with delicate antique furniture, beautiful old-fashioned dresses, hats, shoes, gloves and ribbons. Then they noticed a little girl sitting by the fireplace. Poppy and Honey gasped. It was the same girl they'd seen in the woods. They walked into the room as if in a trance, both overwhelmed by fear and excitement.

"I'm Charlotte de Lafayette," said the girl. She spoke in English, with a heavy French accent.

Poppy and Honey smiled. They couldn't believe what was happening. They'd been right all along – the castle was haunted. But now that they were face to face with a real ghost, all their fear melted away. There was nothing spooky about Charlotte.

Poppy beamed as she looked at the exquisite silk gowns, decorated with ribbons and bows and pretty lace sleeves.

"You can try, if you like," said Charlotte, pointing to the amazing antique dresses and accessories.

But just as Poppy and Honey were deciding which dresses to try on first, they heard Pierre's voice coming from the staircase below.

"*Charlotte, ça va, chérie?*"

He opened the door and the colour drained from his face. "Charlotte! Poppy! Honey!" he said, holding his head in his hands. "Oh no! Everything will have to be

told now! Come with me, girls. I must speak
to your parents, Honey."

"Sorry, Grandfather," said Charlotte as
she went to give Pierre a hug. "I'm so bored
and lonely. There's no one to play with and
I wanted to be friends with these girls. You
and Great-aunt Mathilde and Great-uncle
Jean-Paul are always so busy looking after
the guests."

"Grandfather!" exclaimed Poppy. "But we thought you were the ghost of Charlotte de Lafayette! You're not a ghost at all, are you? Who are you?" she asked, more confused than ever.

Chapter Nine

Pierre assembled everyone in the great
drawing room to explain the mystery of the
child in the turret. Saffron, David, Mr and
Mrs Bumble, Poppy and Honey listened
intently as Pierre began to speak.

"First of all, I have a confession to make.
We are all de Lafayettes. We inherited the
castle but we could not afford to run it
privately so we decided to rent it out for
holidays. Our family has not been wealthy

for many years but we want to keep our
heritage so we work here as servants to
maintain Chateau de Lafayette for future
generations."

Everyone was nodding. This seemed to
make sense so far, although it was a surprise
to discover that the servants were real French
aristocrats.

"I am so sorry about little Charlotte,"
Pierre went on, his arm protectively around
the mysterious little girl, who was so
strikingly similar to the child in the portrait.
"You see, this really is Charlotte de Lafayette,

but not *the* Charlotte de Lafayette. This
Charlotte is my granddaughter and I am
looking after her while my daughter, Aurélie,
finishes her training as a doctor. Charlotte
thinks it is a great game to dress up as her
namesake and spook the guests. She loves
that picture so. I'm afraid she gets bored here
and is inclined to mischief."

Poppy and Honey were struggling to
take in everything they were hearing. It
was almost more exciting than when they'd
thought the castle was haunted! This was a
real-life mystery.

"Poor Charlotte, she must be terribly
lonely," said Mrs Bumble kindly. "It's only

natural for a child to want to dress up, especially with such fabulous costumes!"

"Yes, but I am ashamed to say that we have encouraged her game for the sake of business," sighed Pierre. "You see, we get much interest now because everyone talks of the haunting by sweet little Charlotte de Lafayette. Before this we were struggling to make enough money but now the castle is fully booked. You know how people love to boast about adventurous holidays!"

"So it *is* Charlotte who's been 'haunting' our holiday!" said Poppy as everything finally fell into place.

"Is there no ghost then?" asked Honey, struggling to catch up.

Poppy shook her head. "No, it's a real girl with the same name as the girl in the portrait."

Honey smiled. "Thank goodness!"

"I am so ashamed. I hope very much that

you will be able to forgive us," said Pierre. "You are such nice people – you don't deserve to be deceived."

Daniel Bumble was the first to speak.

"Pierre, you are quite right to preserve your heritage. But it is wrong to mislead and frighten people. I didn't even know the girls suspected that the castle was haunted – they didn't say a word, although they were a bit jumpy. Now it all makes sense."

"We thought you'd say we were imagining it all," said Honey.

Mr Bumble ruffled Honey's hair. "Of course we wouldn't have. You can tell us anything, sweetheart," he said. "Anyway, Pierre, I think this place is plenty big enough for us all. Why not allow Charlotte to play with the girls for the rest of their stay – that should keep her out of mischief!"

"How kind you all are." Pierre smiled. "But I have one question for the girls: how did you find out about the secret passageway?"

"Well, we found a box with Charlotte's initials on it, and inside it was a map and some other stuff," Poppy explained.

"Poppy!" said Pierre. "For years my family has searched for this box! Where did you find it?"

"It was in a secret compartment in the little desk in our bedroom. I'll go and get it," replied Poppy.

She also brought down the book that she'd borrowed from the library on the first day of their holiday. She handed the box to Pierre as well as the book.

"I cannot believe it!" he exclaimed as he opened the box and saw the sealed envelope.

"This is the famous unopened letter from Charlotte to her mother. This has been missing for over two hundred years."

Pierre opened the letter and read it out, translating into English as he went.

Dearest Maman,

Where are you? Why have you left us? I have not seen you for so many days, weeks and months: I try so hard to remember your face and your kind, soft hands, but you are slipping from me now . . .

Please tell me what happened to you after you left to help Her Majesty, Marie Antoinette. I wish you had never gone. I am writing this so that you may find it one day and know how we miss you and love you still.

We have been in hiding here.
Papa says people are angry that we
are so rich. They want to take over
Chateau de Lafayette and throw us out
on the streets. We are all living in
the attic, eating bread and cheese. I
wonder when we will be able to live
normally again - to row on the lake
and picnic in the woods.

Papa has tried to console me but he
does not know how to love us as you do.

I love you, Maman.

kisses,

Charlotte x x x

Poppy felt very sorry for little Charlotte. She
couldn't even imagine life without her mum.
Everyone in the room seemed to be moved
by the letter. Pierre, Mathilde and Jean-Paul
hugged one another. They had been right to

keep Chateau de Lafayette in the family.

"Thank you both for finding this precious letter. We will give it to the local museum. It is an important historical document," said Pierre.

"Pierre?" said Poppy. "Can you tell me what that book is too? I found it in the library, but I can't understand the French words. I think it might have belonged to Charlotte's mother, Marguerite. I mean, the first Charlotte!"

"You're right, Poppy. This is the diary of Marguerite de Lafayette. Shall I read a little extract for you?" replied Pierre as he opened the book towards the beginning.

"Yes please," smiled Poppy.

My children mean everything
to me. They give me such
pleasure. I should hate to be
parted from any of them . . .

"When does the diary end?" asked Mr
Bumble curiously.

"I don't know," replied Pierre sharply and
snapped the book shut. "Anyway, enough
now – yes?"

"Can I look at that book for a minute?"

Reluctantly Pierre passed it to his guest
and Honey's dad read some pages towards
the end of the book.

"This goes on into the eighteen hundreds,
long after the revolution," he said. "It
says here that Marguerite returned to her
children after two years of imprisonment."

"Ah, you have found out another secret.
We knew that Charlotte's mother returned

to Chateau de Lafayette, but guests are more intrigued if they think she was lost during the revolution, so we let them go on believing that. I am sorry. No one ever uncovered our story until Poppy and Honey started doing their detective work! I cannot believe they found the diary too – it is just one little book among hundreds in the library. But the letter the girls found in the desk – we have never seen that, I promise you," concluded Pierre.

Poppy smiled proudly. She was very glad that the first Charlotte had been reunited with her mother. She always liked stories to have happy endings, especially true ones!

"You know what?" laughed Mr Bumble. "I just knew I was going to hit on a great idea for a film while I was here!"

Chapter Ten

Poppy and Honey were pleased that they
had managed to get to the bottom of all
the strange happenings at Chateau de
Lafayette; they were also delighted to have
a new friend to play with for the rest of

their holiday. The three girls had great fun exploring the castle and playing hide and seek in the huge rooms and corridors. They swam in the pool and sketched flowers by the lake and, with Charlotte as their guide, discovered many new places to play. To make everything even more perfect, Poppy's family and Granny Bumble were due to arrive any minute. Poppy couldn't wait. She had so much to tell them.

The next day, when Poppy's mum and dad and little brother and sister had had a good night's sleep after their journey, everyone was busy with the party preparations. No one was allowed to tell Granny Bumble what was going on, so Pierre took her, Poppy, Honey and Charlotte on a trip to Versailles.

"This is where Marie Antoinette, the last French queen, held court," explained Pierre as they bought their tickets. The girls

marvelled at the wonderful ballrooms, ornate
golden furniture and portraits of beautifully
dressed princesses.

"I'd love to try wearing my hair really
high like that!" said Poppy as she looked at
one of the portraits.

"I think I could do that for you, girls,"
laughed Granny Bumble. "I used to have my
hair in a huge beehive like that years ago!"

As the three friends ran around the palace and its gardens, they made believe they were princesses from a bygone era.

"I suppose it was sad for the people who were very poor to see all these riches," said Poppy.

Honey nodded. "It's good to share and not be greedy, isn't it?"

Granny Bumble smiled. She'd had no idea this holiday would teach the girls so much.

That evening, when the girls came down for the party – dressed in fabulous damask silk gowns of powder-blue for Honey, rich raspberry-pink for Poppy and softest green for Charlotte, all with pretty lace and silk roses on the neckline – the adults were already in the ballroom. All three girls looked at each other, then Charlotte smiled and led the way in. The ballroom had a stage at one end and was lined with wonderful paintings of all the de Lafayettes. It was decorated with balloons, streamers and flowers and lit by hundreds of candles. A string chamber orchestra was playing soft music. There was a table laden with food, some of which the girls had helped Mathilde to fetch from the market earlier in the week, and bottles of champagne stood in ice buckets. The girls smiled and Poppy looked at all her family and friends, chatting and laughing. What a wonderful party it was! Then Mrs Bumble told everyone to shush, and Honey's dad led Granny Bumble into the ballroom. Everyone let off a party popper and chorused, "SURPRISE!"

"Oh, I never suspected a thing!" said Granny Bumble. "How lovely! What a surprise!"

Honey's mum had made a special cake for her. "It was a labour of love. I am the

world's worst baker!" She smiled, holding out a slightly flat, wonky sponge cake.

"*C'est magnifique!*" exclaimed Granny Bumble as she tasted a slice. "Nearly as good as my own!"

On the last day of the holiday Poppy and Honey said their goodbyes and invited Charlotte to come and see them in Honeypot Hill one day.

"I will see you next summer!" called Charlotte as they all loaded everything into the car. Then she called out, "Wait a minute. I have something for you."

She ran back inside and appeared with two huge boxes. Inside each was an antique silk dress wrapped in tissue.

"Now your friends will believe your holiday story!" said Charlotte.

"Thank you!" said Poppy as Pierre put the boxes in the car.

"Who knows, maybe we can all be in my dad's movie about the de Lafayettes!" giggled Honey as she and Poppy put on their dark glasses and climbed into the back seat.

THE END

Turn over to read an extract from
the next Princess Poppy book,
The Big Mix-Up . . .

Chapter One

Ever since Poppy's twin brother and sister, Angel and Archie, were born earlier that summer, Poppy's cousin Saffron had been over at Honeysuckle Cottage even more often than usual. Saffron was much older than Poppy, but they were very close. Poppy had been her bridesmaid when Saffron married the village vet, David Sage.

Saffron absolutely adored the twins and spent hours cooing over them. So one day it was decided that Poppy, Mum and Saffron

would do a swap. Saffron would come and
look after the twins for the day while Poppy
and Mum went to work in her shop.
Poppy was thrilled: she had always wanted
to work in the shop because it was so
glamorous – plus it would be nice to have
Mum all to herself for the day!

"I can't wait to be in charge of Saffron's
shop!" Poppy said to herself as she started to
get ready for her big day at work. *What
would a fashion designer wear?* she wondered
as she surveyed all the
clothes in her wardrobe.

Poppy began to try
on outfits, admiring
herself in her long
mirror each time she put
on something different.

"Too party-girl," she
said as she threw a
sparkly dress across her

bed. "Too pony-girl," she decided as she discarded a jeans and wellies combo. Shorts and a T-shirt were "too sporty-girl". She eventually settled on a pretty red skirt and cute white top, with red ankle-strap sandals and a silver sequinned bag. She gathered together everything she thought she might need for the day and put it in her bag: a notebook, coloured pencils, perfume and a hairbrush – it was vital to look good at the shop!

'I'm ready," Poppy called as she raced down the stairs. "Wow! You look *lovely*, Mum!" she said admiringly. Poppy hadn't liked to mention it, but since the twins were born Mum had been looking a bit scruffy.

But today she was wearing a pretty yellow
dress with a wide belt and matching
kitten-heeled shoes. Plus she had put on
pearl earrings *and* make-up!

"Thank you, darling," smiled Mum. "And
you look lovely too."
Just as Mum was wondering where
Saffron had got to, she saw her niece
walking up the garden path and waving at
them cheerily. Poppy rushed to the window
to see what her cousin was wearing —
Saffron had such a great eye for fashion. But
Poppy was rather disappointed by what she

saw. Saffron looked perfectly nice, but what
surprised Poppy was that she looked very . . .
well, ordinary and sensible. For Saffron this
was definitely extraordinary! She was
wearing some old jeans with a loose
emerald-green kaftan top and flat gold
gladiator sandals. Her beautiful red hair was
tied back in a ponytail and she wasn't even
wearing any make-up.

"I'm dressed for childcare!" Saffron
explained as she saw the look on Poppy's
face, which seemed to say, *Why don't you look
as glamorous as usual?* "I've cut my nails short

so that I don't scratch the babies, and I've taken off all my jewellery except my wedding and engagement rings."

"That's very sensible, Saffron," replied Mum. "Angel absolutely loves all things sparkly and shiny – she'd be tugging at your earrings and beads in no time if you hadn't taken them off."

Saffron smiled. She was so excited about looking after the babies, but even though she had spent a lot of time with them since they were born, she was a little nervous – her aunt had always been there, just in case.

"Let's sit down and have a cup of tea and I'll go through everything with you," suggested Mum.

"Thanks, Aunt Lavender," replied Saffron. "I really hope I can manage everything."

"Don't worry, you'll be just fine. Poppy and I have made a list for you so you don't forget anything. Even if you do, you can always give me a ring at the shop," reassured Mum as she unfolded a large piece of paper with writing all over it.

Angel and Archie's Day

9 a.m.: Milk feeds. Mix baby rice with 2oz milk. Spoon feed. Don't forget bibs! Change nappies after breakfast and get the twins dressed. Classical music baby CDs calm them down if they're misbehaving!

10 a.m.: Take for a short walk in pram. Don't forget to take rattles, bottles of sterilized water and spare nappies and wipes just in case.

10.30a.m.: Put the twins down for a nap —
they usually sleep for about
an hour.
While they're sleeping, please
put a wash on & hang up
wet clothes in garden.
Prepare lunch (pureed
carrots, sweet potatoes
and apples).

12p.m.: Lunch, includes milk feed.
<u>Don't forget bibs!</u>

1p.m.: Nappies will probably need
changing and clothes as
well (will be messy from
lunch). Put another
wash on.

1.30p.m.: Walk to shop for fruit
and vegetables, baby
rice and baby bubble
bath — the General Store
has my order, it just
needs collecting.

3 p.m.: Put them down for another nap. Bring in dry washing and hang out wet. Make a start on casserole for supper— ingredients in cupboard and fridge and recipe on fridge. There are lots of toys and a play mat for when twins wake up.

4 p.m.: Prepare the twins' tea and feed them by 5 p.m. (milk feed and porridge).

5.30 p.m.: <u>Bath time</u>. Fill baby baths with bubbles and warm (not hot) water, warm towels on towel rail.

6.30 p.m.: <u>Bed time</u>. Put on new nappies and clean pyjamas and tuck them into their cots. Read a story or sing a lullaby.

Saffron read through the list and gasped. "When will I have my meals and read my Buttons and Bows magazine?" she asked.

Mum laughed. "Try to squeeze your snacks and reading times in during their naps or you'll never eat or relax!" she explained.

Mum took a deep breath. Surely running the shop would be easier than a whole day with the twins.